Nevada Young Readers' Award

North Dakota Children's Choice Award

Nutmeg Children's Book Award (Connecticut)

OMAR Award (Indiana)

Parents' Choice Award

Rebecca Caudill Young Readers' Book Award (Illinois)

Rhode Island Children's Book Award

Sasquatch Reading Award of Washington State

School Library Journal's Best Children's Book of the Year

Tennessee Children's Choice Book Award

Texas Bluebonnet Award

Utah Children's Book Award

West Virginia Honor Book

William Allen White Children's Book Award (Kansas)

Young Hoosier Book Award (Indiana)

BOOKS BY BARBARA PARK:

First chapter books:
The Junie B. Jones series

For middle-grade readers:
Almost Starring Skinnybones
Dear God, Help!!! Love, Earl
Don't Make Me Smile
The Kid in the Red Jacket
Maxie, Rosie, and Earl—Partners in Grime
Mick Harte Was Here
My Mother Got Married (And Other Disasters)
Operation: Dump the Chump
Rosie Swanson: Fourth-Grade Geek for President
Skinnybones

Operation: Dump the Chump

BARBARA PARK

Operation:

Dump the Chump

Barbara Park

Random House 🏠 New York

To Mom and Dad—
Thank you.

Operation:
Dump the Chump

Meet the Chump

I've never really liked my brother. Never. And it's silly to pretend I do.

I keep trying to explain this to my mother, but she doesn't seem to be getting the message. She's always saying stuff like, "Oh, you don't really mean that, Oscar. Deep down inside, you know you love him."

She's wrong, though. Deep down inside, I think the kid's a jerk.

I knew he was going to be a jerk the first day she brought him home from the hospital. I have an excellent memory, so I can remember exactly what happened that morning.

I was watching my favorite cartoon show when my parents walked through the front door. It looked like my mother was carrying a big wad of blue blankets.

Dad was right behind her with the suitcases. He didn't say hello or anything. He just dropped the suitcases and started taping the big "homecoming" with his camcorder.

My mother came into the living room and stood between me and the television. She was grinning from ear to ear. She was also blocking my view of the Roadrunner.

"Oscar," she said, "I've got someone in this blanket who would love to meet you."

I tried to peek around her to see the TV, but my father turned it off.

Mom walked over to the couch and sat down next to me. She rearranged the blankets so I could see the baby's face.

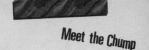

"Oscar Winkle, I would like you to meet your new baby brother, Robert," she said. "Can you say hi to little Robert? Hmm? Can you tell him hello?"

How *insulting*. Of course I could tell him hello. I'd been telling people hello for years. The problem was, I didn't *want* to tell him hello.

"That's dumb," I said. "Why do I have to tell him hello? He's just a baby. He doesn't even understand English."

Mom smiled. "I know he doesn't, Oscar. But I'd still like it if you'd say hi and give him a kiss."

What? Now I had to *kiss* him? I'd never even *met* this kid before.

I took a closer look. His cheeks were all puffy and he didn't have a hair on his head. I would have rather kissed a worm.

My father zoomed in on us with the camera. He started giving directions like some hotshot Hollywood filmmaker.

"Okay, Doris. Put the baby on Oscar's lap. Yes. That's good. That's perfect.

"Okay, Oscar. Now lean over the baby's head and get ready to kiss him."

Oh, my gosh. He was really going to make me *do* this.

I looked down at Robert again.

Something about him looked different. His face was getting redder and redder. And he was getting this totally weird grin on his face.

All of a sudden, he began making all these disgusting grunting noises. It didn't take a genius to figure out what he was doing.

Gross! I *had* to get him off my lap!

Quickly, I stood up.

When I did, Robert landed on the floor.

He wasn't hurt or anything. How could he be hurt with all those blankets around him? But he started to scream his head off anyway.

The next thing I knew, my father had grabbed me by the arm and was marching me to my room. I still can't believe he did that. Robert goes to the bathroom while he's right on my lap, and *I'm* the one who gets punished. Yeah, that's fair.

Right then and there, I knew the kid was going to be a jerk.

I've been correct about him, too. Robert is

almost eight now, and every year he's gotten jerkier.

I used to hope that when he started school, he'd mature a little bit. But school has only made Robert worse. I was a lot better off before he ever learned how to read or write.

Last Christmas was the perfect example of what can happen when a jerky kid gets educated. I'll never forget it. For the first time ever, I had decided to send my own Christmas cards to my friends. My dad even took me to the card store and let me pick out any box I wanted.

I swear I must have looked at every single card in the place. But finally, I decided on a box of funny ones. On the front of the cards was this happy Santa with an elf sitting on his head. Santa was saying, "MERRY CHRISTMAS, _____!" You were supposed to fill in the blank space with the name of the person you were sending it to.

As soon as I got home that day, I hurried to show them to my mother.

"I'm home! I'm home!" I shouted as I ran in the front door. "Wait till you see the cards I picked out, Mom! They're great!"

"I just got in the tub, Oscar!" my mother yelled back. "Leave them on the table and I'll look at them as soon as I get out."

I put my new box of cards on the kitchen table and went to watch TV.

Thirty minutes later, when Mom came out of the bathroom, I rushed to the kitchen to get them.

But the cards were gone.

It didn't take long to find them, though. All I had to do was look in Robert's room.

There they were, spread out all over his bed. He had taken every single one of them and printed the words "POOPOO HED" in the spaces where the names were supposed to go.

I was so mad I thought I would explode.

I ran into the bedroom to show my mother. "Look what that little creep wrote all over my new cards!" I hollered. "They're ruined! They're ruined!"

My mother looked at the cards. "'Merry Christmas, Poopoo Hed,'" she read out loud.

She kept her head down for a very long time. It was pretty clear that she was trying to keep herself from laughing.

Finally, she looked up. "He spelled *head* wrong," she said.

I couldn't believe it! My jerky brother ruined my new Christmas cards, and all my mother could do was correct his spelling!

"Geez, Mother! This isn't a spelling bee!" I snapped. "Aren't you going to do something?"

Mom called Robert into her room. He had been hiding in his closet. She scolded him and said he'd have to use his own money to buy me a new box of cards.

I mean, that was *it*. That was his *entire* punishment.

If you ask me, she should have put him back in his closet and made him stay there until Christmas was over!

Of course, Christmas isn't the only holiday that Robert has ruined for me. Over the past few years, he has managed to ruin Easter, Halloween, Thanksgiving, Valentine's Day, the Fourth of July, and my birthday. In fact, until a couple of months ago, I thought that Robert had ruined every holiday possible. I was wrong, though. This year, he even managed to ruin my school field trip . . . which isn't a holiday, exactly, but it's close enough for me.

It happened in April. Our class was going to the city to visit the Museum of Natural History. I was really looking forward to it, too. Except for the dentist, I look forward to almost anything that gets me out of doing schoolwork.

A week before the trip, my teacher sent a note home asking parents to pack their kids sack lunches and put our names on the front. It seemed like a pretty harmless request. But with a creep like Robert in the family, a harmless request can turn into disaster.

On the morning of the field trip, my mother packed the biggest lunch you ever saw. She was trying to be nice by packing extra chips and stuff. But there were so many little "treats," the food wouldn't even fit into a regular lunch sack, so Mom had to pack it in a big brown grocery bag. It was the most humiliating lunch bag I ever saw in my life.

As soon as she was out of the room, I rolled down the sides of the bag and tried to make it look

as small as I could. But no matter what I did, it still looked like a giant grocery sack.

Then, as if that wasn't bad enough, my mother came back with a big black marker and printed "OSCAR T. WINKLE" on the front of the bag in capital letters.

Oh, good. Perfect. Now, even from miles away, people would be able to see that the world's stupidest lunch bag belonged to me.

As soon as she finished, Robert came walking into the kitchen. He stared at the bag for a second, then started laughing his head off. He couldn't stop.

At first, I thought he was just laughing at the size of it. But after a minute, he pointed at my name on the bag.

"Oscar *T.* Winkle!" he roared. "Wow. How come I never even noticed that before? Your middle initial turns *Winkle* into *Twinkle.*"

After that, his hysterics got even louder. "*Twinkle!* Ha! That's kind of a cute little nickname, don't you think, Twink? Just wait till your friends on the bus see that! They're gonna *love* it."

Eventually, my mother sent him out of the

room. I think she was mad because he was making fun of her sack. But it was too late. The damage had already been done.

Robert had made me so nervous about my lunch bag that I put it inside another—even bigger—bag to hide my name.

When I finally carried it onto the bus that morning, the driver asked if I thought we were going on a two-week safari. Even my teacher cracked up at that one.

Humiliating me. That's Robert's mission in life. If you don't know what it means to humiliate someone, I'll give you an example. Humiliation is what you feel when your brother takes your athletic supporter to school for show-and-tell. I know. Robert's done it.

As a matter of fact, Robert has done almost every jerky thing you can think of. But a guy like me can only stand so much. After that, he gets fed up and he starts taking things into his own hands.

That's just what I did when I created my plan to get rid of Robert.

I called it Operation: Dump the Chump.

Step Number One—

Robert
Needs
a Home

We live on the kind of street that you see on TV commercials sometimes. You know, the kind with lots of shady oak trees and houses with screened-in porches. It's a pretty good place to live, probably. But when you have to live with Robert, no place seems that great.

There's an older couple who lives on the corner. Mr. Henson is about eighty, I think, but he's still in pretty good shape. He really likes kids, too.

When Robert and I were younger, we'd go down there on Saturdays and Mr. Henson would give us rides in his wheelbarrow.

Sometimes when Mr. Henson smiles, he doesn't have his false teeth in and you can see his gums. You don't want to look, but your eyes keep going there.

I don't like saying mean stuff about such a nice man, but there's something else that bothers me about Mr. Henson, too. He's got a bunch of wiry gray hairs growing out of his ears. I don't know why he doesn't just clip them off. If he clipped them off, his ears would be a whole lot easier to look at.

Mrs. Henson is a few years younger than Mr. Henson, I think. It's hard to tell, but I figure she's only about seventy-five. Or who knows? Maybe she just seems younger because she still wears shorts. Her knees are kind of saggy, but Mrs. Henson just jokes about them.

Almost nothing seems to bother Mrs. Henson. I guess that's why she's never gotten Mr. Henson to clip his ear hairs. One time, I saw her pick up a dead bird and put it in her trash can. She didn't even have gloves on, I mean.

Nope. Almost nothing bothers Mrs. Henson at all. Not even Robert. Which is *exactly* why the Hensons were going to be such an important part of Operation: Dump the Chump.

They didn't know it, of course. My plan was *top-secret*. But without the Hensons, there would be no plan at all. So I had to be very careful how I handled them.

The first step of Operation: Dump the Chump was extremely important. I was going to need to have a serious conversation with Mr. Henson about Robert. But the timing of the conversation had to be perfect. So while I waited for the right moment, I spent my time rehearsing exactly what I would say.

My patience finally paid off. It was the second Saturday in May, and the sun was shining bright. It was a warm day—but not hot—so I was almost positive Mr. Henson would be outside working in his garden. Also, Robert would be at baseball practice for at least two hours. So there was no way he could interfere with what I was about to do.

My heart was pounding with excitement as I started out the front door. "I'm going out for a while, Mom! I'll be home later!" I shouted.

She shouted something back.

I stopped. "What? What did you say?"

"I asked you where you were going," she called.

"I don't know, Mom. Just around," I answered.

"Just around *where,* Oscar?"

Geez! I hate it when my mother nags me like that. It's like I have to report every little move I make. Just once, I wish she would say, "I don't care where you go or what you do, Oscar. It's none of my business. Just have fun and come home whenever you feel like it."

"Did you hear the question, Oscar?" my mother shouted again. "Around where?"

"I'm not *sure* where," I hollered. "Just around outside somewhere."

Even though this still didn't tell her where I'd be, for some reason she seemed satisfied.

"Okay, bye!" she called.

Mothers. Man. What goes on in their brains?

I left the house and headed straight for the Hensons. When I got there, Mr. Henson was out front weeding his vegetable garden, just like I thought.

I walked up his driveway. "Hi, Mr. Henson," I said.

He looked up and smiled. He didn't have his teeth in.

"Why, hello there, young fella," he said back.

Mr. Henson almost always calls me *young fella*. I have a feeling it's because he doesn't really like the name *Oscar* that much.

"What'cha up to today?" he asked.

I hesitated a second. "Oh, nothing much," I said. "I've just been walking around. You know . . . just thinking about stuff."

"Just thinking about stuff, huh?" he repeated. "How's that little brother of yours?"

Aha! This was *exactly* the question I'd been hoping for. I was pretty sure he'd ask it, too. Whenever I'm alone, Mr. Henson almost always asks me about Robert.

I stalled a little more. "Well, the thing is, Mr. Henson, I would like to tell you about Robert, but I'm not allowed. My parents made me promise not to discuss the situation with the neighbors."

Mr. Henson shrugged. "Okay, then," he said. "Let's talk about the World Series instead. Who looks good to you this year?"

I could *not* believe this. What the heck was wrong with Mr. Henson, anyway? There I was, dangling a big, fat family secret right in front of his face, and all he could ask me about was the World Series?

Somehow, I had to get him to ask me about Robert again.

"Gee, I don't really know who looks good this year, Mr. Henson," I said. "Like I mentioned a minute ago, we sort of have a *situation* at home with Robert right now. So it's been kind of hard to concentrate on anything else."

I swear I'm not making this up. Mr. Henson said, "Oh, well. It's probably too early to start talking about the World Series, anyway."

I just couldn't *stand* it.

"For gosh sake, Mr. Henson!" I blurted out. "Haven't you heard a word I said? Don't you even *care* what's happening to Robert? Robert's always liked you, Mr. Henson. And I've liked you, too. But now, when poor little Robert's in trouble, you act like it doesn't matter."

Mr. Henson looked shocked.

"Whoa, whoa, whoa! Hold on there, young fella," he said. "Just simmer down. I didn't want to pry into your family business, that's all. But if you have something you really want to tell me, I'm listening. Has something happened to Robert? Is it something you think I need to know about?"

Ah . . . now, this was more like it!

"Okay, Mr. Henson. Fine," I said. "If you insist on pulling my secret out of me, I guess I'll have to tell you."

I took a deep breath. "Last night, my father came home from work with the worst news I ever heard."

"What kind of news?" he asked. "What *was* it?"

My shoulders slumped. "My father got fired from his job yesterday," I said.

Mr. Henson's hand went over his mouth. *"No,"* he said. "What happened?"

I shook my head. "I don't know all the details, Mr. Henson," I said. "All I know for sure is that my dad's boss has never really liked him that much. And yesterday he walked into my father's office and he gave Dad the boot. He *canned* him, Mr. Henson. With no warning or anything."

Mr. Henson walked to his porch and sat down on the step.

"Good heavens. That's terrible, young fella," he said. "That's awful."

He was quiet a minute. "But wait. I thought you said you were having a situation at home with *Robert,*" he said.

"Yeah, well, I was just getting to that part," I said. "See, after my father finished telling us the bad news, he went up to his room to cry his eyes out or something. And that's when my mother told Robert and me that she was almost out of grocery money. She said that when school got out, she might have to send us to Grandma Winkle's for the summer."

Mr. Henson nodded. "All right. Okay. I guess that makes sense."

"Yeah, sort of," I said. "But then I reminded Mom about what a big help I am around the house and all. Plus I happen to eat like a bird, Mr. Henson. And if a family wants to cut down on their food bills, it's the pig of the family that's gotta go. And believe me, in our family, the piggo is Robert."

I paused. "Besides that, Robert's bedroom is a lot bigger than mine, so we can rent it out for the summer. That's why Mom finally decided that only Robert needed to go," I said. "But when she called Grandma Winkle, she found out that my grandmother is off on a cruise somewhere. So who knows where the heck poor Robert will end up now?"

I sighed. "It's not that any of us *want* Robert to leave, you understand. It's just that Robert is a big pig with a huge room."

I walked over to the garden.

"Whoa. Look at all these vegetables you've planted, Mr. Henson," I said. "I bet you've planted enough vegetables to feed a whole *army* of kids.

I'll have to bring Robert over here and let him see your garden. Boy, does that kid ever love home-grown tomatoes."

Mr. Henson smiled a little. His smile didn't last long, though. He was seriously upset.

"But don't you think your father will be able to get another job soon?" he asked me. "He works at the bank, doesn't he? Surely there must be other banking jobs available. Or how about your mother? Maybe your mother can go to work for a while to help out."

To tell you the truth, even though I had planned Step Number One pretty carefully, I hadn't really expected Mr. Henson to ask a bunch of questions like this.

I sputtered around, trying to make up answers.

"Uh, well, see . . . my father's boss is friends with all the other banks in town. So he called all his pals and he told them Dad's a troublemaker. And as for my mother, she'd definitely work if she could, but Mom's got a bum . . . knee."

Mr. Henson frowned. "What about savings,

then? Didn't your father have any savings for an emergency? Or relatives? Couldn't he borrow money from his family?"

For Pete's sake. Why wouldn't he stop?

"Yes, well, um . . . my father *used* to have some savings," I went on. "But we think that Grandma Winkle stole it to pay for her cruise. We don't know how, exactly. But Grandma's always been a little bit on the *shady* side, if you know what I mean."

Mr. Henson just stared at me. I wasn't sure if he believed me or not, but I had to keep going.

"And as for my father's other relatives, well, you probably won't believe this, Mr. Henson, but my father is the only one in his family who has ever *had* a job. He has two brothers, but they're both drifters. They live out in the desert some-where, I think."

"Oh, dear," said Mr. Henson. "This is worse than I thought. Your poor, poor family."

"Yeah. It's poor, poor us, all right," I said. "And it's especially poor, poor Robert. I mean, I'm sure my mother will find a nice place for Robert to stay and all. But still, it's too bad that there's no one right here in the neighborhood who would like to keep the little guy for a while."

I waited for a minute to make sure he'd heard that part. "Poor little Robert. The kid's a real joy, you know?"

Finally, I stood up and started for home. "Okay. Well, thanks for listening, Mr. Henson," I said. "I'd better be getting home now. My poor mother's probably wondering where I am. I think we're supposed to paint Robert's room today. That way, it'll be easier to rent."

I walked a few steps, then turned around. "Remember, Mr. Henson. Don't say one word about this to anyone, okay? And *especially* don't mention it to Robert or my parents. I'll get in a lot of trouble if they ever find out that I've told you our problems."

Mr. Henson waved his hand. "Oh, you don't need to worry about me, young fella," he said. "I won't make things harder for you."

After that, he went up the porch steps and into the house.

As soon as he was out of sight, I jumped high in the air. After weeks of planning, the first step of Operation: Dump the Chump was complete!

And if you ask me, it had gone pretty darned well!

Step Number Two—

Hensons Need a Boy

I went straight home to get ready for Step Number Two. Even though my conversation with Mr. Henson had gone so well, I needed time to think things through. If I rushed the next step before I was ready, I could blow the whole plan.

My mother must have heard the door slam. She called to me from the kitchen. "Oscar? Why are you home so soon? What's wrong?"

"Nothing's wrong," I hollered back. "Just nothing to do, that's all. I'm going up to my room for a while."

"But why?" Mom called again. "Don't you feel well? Are you sick?"

This is another thing that kills me about my mother. Whenever I want to stay inside on a Saturday, she automatically thinks I'm sick. It just doesn't make sense. If being inside on Saturday means you're sick, then my mother must be sick every weekend.

"I feel fine, Mom," I said. "*Really*. I feel perfect."

I ran up to my room and locked the door behind me. Then I checked the closet to make sure Robert wasn't hiding in there. Also, I checked the windows to make sure he wasn't spying on me. Checking the windows might sound kind of extreme when your room is on the second floor. But with a sneak like Robert, you can't be too careful.

To show you what I mean, last September when school started, my mother went to the store to buy me some new underwear. When she came back, she asked me to try it on to make sure it was the right size.

I didn't want to. But in third grade she had bought me underwear that was way too big. And when I climbed the rope in P.E., Joanne Reilly told the whole gym class that she could look up my shorts and see my "wares." I'm still not sure what that means, exactly. But ever since then, I've tried on new underpants whenever Mom has asked.

Anyhow, I was up in my room trying on the new underwear that day when I happened to catch a glimpse of myself in the dresser mirror. And to tell you the truth, I didn't look too bad.

I got the chair from my desk and put it in front of my dresser. Then, totally goofing around, I stood on the chair and began flexing. You know, like those bodybuilders do.

That's when I heard it.

A loud scream of laughter practically shattered the air.

I spun around.

There, standing on a ladder looking in my second-floor window, was dumb, jerk-o Robert!

"VA-VA-VA-VOOM!" he roared. Then he

started whistling and hooting like you wouldn't believe.

I was so shocked and angry, I must have gone crazy for a minute. Because the next thing I knew, I was running down the stairs, out the front door, and straight into the yard.

I caught Robert just as he was climbing down from the ladder. I pulled him the rest of the way off. Then I clobbered him as hard as I could.

He screamed so loud that Mr. and Mrs. Farley from next door came running over to see what was the matter.

That's when I realized that I was still in my underwear.

It was one of the worst moments of my life. I didn't know what to do or say . . . and neither did the Farleys. So the three of us kept standing there looking at each other until the awkwardness got so terrible, I couldn't stand it anymore.

Finally, I just kind of waved. "Sooo . . . Mr. and Mrs. Farley . . . how do you like my new tidy whities?" I said stupidly.

Mrs. Farley rolled her eyes in disgust and

went back to her house. Meanwhile, Mr. Farley frowned.

"Don't you think you're a little old to be parading around the neighborhood in your panties, Oscar?" he said.

I'm serious. The guy called my underwear *panties*.

I've never really forgiven Mr. Farley for that.

When I finally got back inside, my mother followed me around for the next hour or two, yelling about how I was "one of those kids who don't even *deserve* new underpants." Whatever that means.

Anyhow, the point of the story is that when you have a brother like Robert, you've got to be on your toes every minute. Which is why I checked the closet and the windows before I took out my secret notebook with the plans for Operation: Dump the Chump.

When I was sure the coast was clear, I sat down on my bed and opened it to the first page. Then I took a pencil and made a check mark beside Step Number One.

I looked over the rest of the steps. There were eight of them in all:

Operation: Dump the Chump
Step #1: Tell Hensons that Robert needs a home. ✓
Step #2: Tell parents that Hensons need a boy.
Step #3: Put fake ad in paper from Hensons.
Step #4: Show ad to parents.
Step #5: Put fake ad in paper from parents.
Step #6: Show ad to Hensons.
Step #7: Write fake letter to Hensons.
Step #8: Write fake letter to parents.

My stomach flip-flopped in anticipation. "You're a genius, Oscar Winkle," I whispered. "A genuine, actual genius."

I reread the first two steps. Now that I had told Mr. Henson the story about Robert, it was time to tell my mother the story about the Hensons. This time, though, I would have to be prepared for *anything*. If Mom put her mind to it, she could think of a million more questions than Mr. Henson ever could.

I got to work again. First, I went over exactly what I would say. Next, I made a list of every possible question that I thought my mother might come up with.

I had been working in my room for over an hour when she called me to come down for lunch.

I took a deep breath. This was it. I was ready.

I walked into the kitchen and looked all around. "Where's Robert?" I asked, casual as anything.

"Oh, he called and asked if he could eat over at the Bradfords'," said Mom. "He won't be home till later."

Perfect! I had her all to myself. But even so, I didn't start right in talking. Instead, I ate my sandwich in complete silence. I didn't even look up from my plate, I mean.

My mother was eating across from me. "You're awfully quiet today, Oscar," she said. "Are you *sure* something isn't the matter?"

Yes! I knew she would ask me that! I had even *counted* on it. She was still convinced I was sick.

I sighed. "No. Nothing's *wrong,* exactly," I said.

"I was just sitting here thinking about poor old Mrs. Henson, that's all."

Mom raised her eyebrows.

"Mrs. Henson? You mean Mrs. Henson who lives at the corner? What's wrong with her? Did something happen?" she asked.

"No. Not really," I said. "It's just that I saw her while I was outside this morning. And she told me about some problems she's been having lately."

"Like what kind of problems?" asked Mom.

I shrugged. "I don't know. Mostly they're problems with *Mr.* Henson," I said. "She said that Mr. Henson is getting older now, and it's making things hard on her."

Mom kept on. "But why, though? Did he fall? Is he ill?"

"No, he's not ill, exactly," I answered. "And I don't think he fell, either. Mrs. Henson said that he's just not as peppy as he used to be, so she ends up doing most of the work around the house."

"Was she upset?" she asked next.

"Kind of," I said. "She kept holding her back and saying how nice it would be if she had a live-in helper. You know, like a nice little grandson or someone who could help her with the raking and stuff. She said she'd like to hire someone, but they don't have the money."

Mom frowned. "That's odd," she said. "They had the money to fly to Hawaii last year."

Oh, man! I could have kicked myself. I had totally forgotten about the Hensons' trip to Hawaii.

I started stuttering. "Uh, yeah, well, Mrs. Henson said that the Hawaii trip was part of the problem. I think she said that while they were over there, Mr. Henson's sister stole their life savings or something."

My mother got a strange expression. "*What?* How could that happen?"

I hurried on to another subject. "I don't know, Mom. I didn't get all the details. All I know for sure is that Mrs. Henson needs help. She said that her tired old back can't hold up much longer if she has to keep dragging Mr. Henson around like she does."

"Dragging him around? What do you mean dragging him around?"

I had a feeling that part would get to her.

"Well, I've never actually seen her do it," I said. "But Mrs. Henson said that sometimes when Mr. Henson gets really tired in his garden, she has to drag him through the yard to get him back to the house. And at night—if Mr. Henson is totally pooped—she sort of *piggybacks* him upstairs to bed."

My mother looked stunned. "*Piggybacks* him?" she repeated. "No. I can't believe that, Oscar. I just saw Mr. Henson working in his garden this morning. He looked perfectly healthy."

"Yeah, well, that's because Mr. Henson has good days and bad days," I explained. "Mrs. Henson said that one day last week he took a nap in his garden and he squished a whole row of squash."

Quickly, I got up from the table. The second step of Operation: Dump the Chump was almost finished, and I couldn't risk any more questions.

Just one other thing needed to be said.

On my way out the door, I mumbled something about Robert.

"What? What was that?" Mom asked.

"Oh, nothing," I said. "I just keep thinking

about how much Robert has always liked the Hensons. And it's funny, too, because the Hensons practically *love* Robert. Do you know what Mrs. Henson said when I was leaving today, Mom? She said, 'Oscar, please don't tell your family what I've just told you. I don't want to worry them. And, most of all, don't tell Robert. I love that little boy like a grandson. He's such a joy, that Robert is.'"

I paused to let it sink in. "That's what she called him, Mother. Mrs. Henson called Robert a *joy*."

After that, I opened the screen door and headed outside. "I'm going to walk down to the Hensons' and make sure everything's okay," I said. "See you later, Mom."

As soon as I hit the sidewalk, I took off running.

I just couldn't help myself, you know? The excitement was about to explode right out of me.

Halfway down the block, I jumped into the air again.

"YEEE-HAAA!"

Two steps down and six to go.

Then it was good-bye, Robert the Slobert!

Step Number Three—

The
Personals

The next day was Sunday. To me, Sunday is the most boring day of the week. I don't know what makes it so different from Saturday. But Sunday feels dull from the time I wake up.

My mother always fixes a special big breakfast on Sunday morning. She calls it our family's "quality time" together. You know . . . as if eating a pancake across from Robert is going to make me like him better.

A lot of kids go to church on Sundays. Robert and I tried that for a while, but it didn't actually work out that well. Mom signed us up for Sunday school at church down the street. She said we would have a lot of fun and we'd learn about the Bible. But all I really learned was that I stink at art.

Mostly, I blame it on our Sunday school teacher. I'm sure there are tons of Sunday school teachers better than ours was. But Robert and I definitely got stuck with a lemon.

Her name was Mrs. Blesshu. She pronounced it like the words *bless you,* which is probably the only reason she became a Sunday school teacher in the first place.

Every week, Mrs. Blesshu would walk into the room and pass out Bible pictures for us to color. Then she'd put this box of old broken crayons on the table and tell us to "get busy." Most of the crayons were so little, you couldn't get a good grip on them, so your picture ended up looking like scribble.

When we finished coloring, there was always an arts-and-crafts project for us to work on. The trouble was, all of the projects were designed for three-year-olds. The first week, we had to make a church out of a little milk carton. Unfortunately, I colored my church red, so it ended up looking like a little barn.

When Mrs. Blesshu saw it, she said I shouldn't be making a joke out of "God's house." I didn't try to defend myself. I'd rather let her think I was a smart aleck than to admit that I actually like red churches. But after that, I wasn't too excited about going back to Sunday school anymore.

Robert didn't get along with Mrs. Blesshu any better than I did. He's the one who got us kicked out. One Sunday, we were supposed to color a picture of baby Jesus and then draw a halo around his head. The class had just started working on it when—all of a sudden—Mrs. Blesshu grabbed Robert's picture away from him and put it in the trash. She took away his crayons and made him sit at the table all by himself.

As soon as she wasn't looking, I went over and got Robert's crumpled picture out of the trash can to see what he had done. Instead of drawing a halo, Robert had put a top hat on the baby's head. The kind of hat that Frosty the Snowman wears.

I have to admit, the picture was pretty amusing. I have a feeling that God has a good sense of humor about kids and the dumb stuff they do. Like I'm almost positive that he made Robert as a joke, for instance.

Anyway, our teacher didn't let Robert work on the arts-and-crafts project that week. We were making halos, and I guess she figured that he didn't deserve one. When my mother came to pick us up that morning, I heard Mrs. Blesshu tell her that she didn't think Robert should come back unless he could behave better.

Mom was totally embarrassed, of course. She yelled at Robert for a really long time. Then she told us that we couldn't go back to Sunday school until we got more mature. She sincerely thought that she was punishing us.

On Sunday, Robert gets on my nerves more than any other day of the week. He does it on purpose, too. He begins the minute that I get up from the breakfast table. As soon as I head upstairs to get dressed, he's right on my heels. Then—even though I lock him out of my room—he sits in the hall and pretends he can see me undressing through the crack under the door. I always block it with something, so I know that he can't. But just to show you what a jerk he is, every week Robert still whistles and claps like he's watching me change my clothes. The kid's an idiot, I'm telling you.

After I'm dressed, I go back down to the kitchen and start complaining that there's nothing to do. Eventually, Mom gets fed up and sends me outside.

That's when Robert starts spying. I'm serious. No matter where I go in the yard, he hides in the bushes and peeks at me. Robert's the worst spy in the world, too. Sometimes he hides behind trees that are so skinny, the whole world can see him and he doesn't even know it.

Anyhow, the Sunday after I began Operation: Dump the Chump, I finally decided to teach him a lesson.

After breakfast, I went outside and sat down

on the porch steps. It wasn't long before I heard Robert crawling through the bushes on the side of the house. He was about as quiet as a bulldozer.

At first, I just sat there pretending I couldn't hear him. Then I got up and started wandering around the yard. I acted as if I was looking for something I'd lost. Every once in a while, I would stoop over and search around in my mother's flower bed.

Finally, casual as anything, I strolled over to the bushes where Robert was hiding. . . .

And I started to spit.

I'm not kidding. I stood right in front of the bushes, and I spit like I had never spit before!

Robert came flying out!

"HEY! QUIT IT! KNOCK IT OFF! I'M TELLIN' MOM!" he shouted. Then he ran straight into the house.

Within seconds, he was back outside with my mother.

She was furious. "Oscar! For heaven's sakes! How could you do that? How could you *spit* on your brother?" she said.

"I *didn't*, Mother," I said. "I swear I didn't spit on anyone. I was spitting on the bushes."

"No, you weren't!" yelled Robert. "You were spitting on *me!*" He pointed at two little spit blobs on his shoulder. "If this isn't spit, then what do you call it?"

I examined it closer. "Slobert," I said with a straight face.

I thought this was a pretty witty thing to say. But my mother looked like she wanted to kill me.

"Come on, Mom. It was an *accident*," I insisted. "I was just practicing my spitting technique on the bushes. A guy's gotta learn how to spit, you know. And besides, if you want to yell at someone, yell at Robert for spying on me. If he hadn't been hiding in there, he wouldn't have been in the line of fire."

I guess my mother wasn't in the mood to decide who was right or wrong, because Robert and I both got sent to our rooms. But even so, seeing his shirt with those two spit blobs was definitely worth the punishment.

Besides, being in my room gave me time to work on the third step of Operation: Dump the

Chump without worrying about Robert the Sneak.

I took out my secret notebook and read out loud, "'Step Number Three: Put fake ad in paper from Hensons.'"

Since I had never written an ad before, I was definitely going to need some help on this one.

I went downstairs and asked my mother if I could borrow the Sunday paper. I told her I wanted to read it while I was up in my room being punished. I'm sure she wondered why, but she let me have it without a lot of questions.

I went back to my room and locked my door. Then I opened the paper up to the classified ads section. Classified ads are ads that people write when they want or need something special—like if you want to hire someone for a special job. Or if you want to sell something that you don't want anymore.

As I read the ads, I noticed that most of them were only a couple of lines long. Maybe this wasn't going to be as hard as I thought.

At the bottom of the page, I found a telephone number to call if you wanted to put an ad in the paper. Amazing. All I would have to do was write a few lines and phone them in.

I went over to my desk and began writing some samples of how the ad should sound. I don't know how long I worked that morning, but finally, the wording sounded pretty good.

NEEDED: Nice young man to help old couple. Will provide room and board. Call 555-3447.

I smiled proudly. It sounded as if the Hensons had actually written it themselves.

The very next morning, I called the paper. I told the lady who answered that I wanted to place an ad in next Sunday's paper. It was so simple, I could hardly believe it! All I did was read her my ad over the phone. And that was that.

She said that my ad would go in the personals section. I told her she could put it wherever she wanted to, just as long as it was in next Sunday's paper.

Before she hung up, the newspaper lady asked me how I wanted to pay for it.

"How much is it?" I asked.

"Six dollars," she said. "If you like, you can stop at our business office before Wednesday and pay for it. Or, if you prefer, we can send you a bill."

A *bill*? No way. If my mother ever saw a newspaper bill addressed to me, my whole plan would be ruined.

"No. *Please*. No bills, okay? I'm too young for bills," I said. "I'll ride my bike to your office after school."

The lady laughed and told me where the office was located. It was right across the street from the post office, so I knew I would have no trouble finding it.

After I hung up, I went to my bank and stuffed six dollars into my jeans.

I told my mother I would be late getting home from school that day. I said I was working on a very big project.

I wasn't lying, either. Operation: Dump the Chump was the biggest project of my life.

Step Number Four—

Sunday Paper: Page Six!

The week dragged on forever. Every day, I pulled out my notebook and reread the fourth step of my plan: "Show ad to parents." All I could think about was my ad being in the Sunday paper and how it would look.

This step was definitely one of the most important steps of the plan. Somehow, I was going to have to make my parents believe that the ad I'd put in the paper had been written by the Hensons. So, just like before, I went over and over a million different questions they might have. But as it turned out, it was easier than I thought.

When Sunday finally came again, I went down to breakfast the same as usual. Naturally, Robert was already at the table, gulping down his juice like a slob.

"Morning," I said to my parents.

I looked at Robert.

"Morning, dribble-puss," I said.

My father gave me the look he always does when he thinks a fight is about to break out. "Don't start," he said.

My mother had just begun making the pancakes, so breakfast was going a little slow. It was torture sitting there trying to act normal. Inside, I was so nervous about my ad, I could hardly stand it.

Robert was blabbing on and on about how good his baseball team was doing. This wouldn't have been so bad. But at least twice he added how glad he was that he wasn't on a P.U. team like mine.

"Will someone please tell Robert to shut up?"

I said finally. "If anyone knows anything about P.U., it's you, Robert. You're so P.U., I can smell your fumes from here."

Dad rustled his paper. He didn't yell, though. At our house, my mother is in charge of most of the morning yelling.

"If I hear one more word, both of you are going to leave the table without your pancakes," she said.

I was getting hungry by then, so I decided to shut up. Robert wasn't as smart.

After a couple of minutes, he started sniffing the air. "Pew," he said. "Whose baseball team stinks?"

I think he only said it to see if my mother meant business.

She did.

He was gone in a flash.

When the pancakes were finally ready, Dad put the paper down on the counter and we all dug in. But the whole time I was eating, my heart was beating like crazy. I knew that my ad was somewhere in the paper right next to where I was sitting. And the tension was really getting to me.

After I finished eating, I asked if I could take the paper up to my room to read again.

"What's all this sudden interest in reading the paper?" my mother asked. "Is this an assignment for school or something?"

I kept my voice calm. "No, not really," I said. "I'm just developing an interest in the news and stuff, sort of."

Man, were my parents impressed with *that* one.

"Well, good for you!" said my father. "Looks like you're finally growing up, Oscar."

I know my dad meant well and all. But comments like that annoy me, if you want to know the truth. Whenever I do something good, he says it's because I'm growing up. Is it totally impossible to think I could do something good and still be a kid?

Anyway, after I got the paper, I went straight to my room and found the classified ads. There must have been about a million ads in the paper that day. But after about twenty minutes, I finally found the personals at the bottom of page six.

And what do you know? There it was!

**NEEDED: Nice young man to help old couple. Will
provide room and board. Call 555-3447.**

Yes! It was perfect! Even the phone number
was just the way I had written it. Naturally, I
wasn't able to use the Hensons' *real* phone number in the ad. I mean, I didn't want anyone actually
calling their house or anything. So when I wrote
the ad, I changed the last number. The Hensons'
real phone number is 555-344*6*. But in the ad, I
had put 555-344*7*.

Brilliant, huh? I wondered what the poor
people with the 3447 number would think when a
bunch of "nice young men" started calling for a job.

I stayed in my room a few more minutes, just
staring at my ad. But finally, I knew it was time to
carry out Step Number Four.

I took some deep breaths and braced myself.
Then I headed back downstairs.

My parents were still in the kitchen, having
their fiftieth cup of coffee.

I hurried in. "Mom! Oh, my gosh. You're not going to *believe* this!" I said.

"Believe what?" she asked.

I opened the paper and pointed. "I was just looking through the ads to see if there was any cheap stuff for sale and look what I found!"

I held out the ad for her to see.

"'NEEDED: Nice young man to help old couple,'" she read.

Then she looked over at me and said, "So what?"

"So *what*?" I asked. "So don't you remember what I told you about the you-know-whos down the street?"

When my father heard me say "you-know-whos," he glanced up.

"What in the world are you two talking about?" he asked. He sounded a little bit hurt. Sometimes I think I should tell my father more secrets, just so he'll feel like he's part of the family.

After that, my mother filled him in on all the things I had told her about the Hensons. Then, together, they took a closer look at my ad. They reread it several times.

"Oh, those poor sweet old people," said my mother. "I just feel so sorry for them. Imagine, having to advertise for a boy to come and live with them. This is just so sad."

My father frowned. "But wait a minute," he said. "We don't even know for sure that the Hensons placed this ad. Maybe it was some other old couple."

I *knew* my father would say something like this. He always doubts everything. But this time, I was ready.

"So maybe we should check the phone number," I said. "If it's the Hensons' number, that will prove it."

My mother got the phone book and looked up the Hensons' number. She checked it against the ad.

"Oh, dear," she said. "It looks like it's the Hensons' number, all right. The paper made a mistake and printed a seven instead of a six. But all the other numbers are exactly the same. I'm sure the Hensons must have placed that ad."

After that, Mom kept going on and on about how sad it was that they had no one to help them. It was so *amazing,* I couldn't stand it.

I started for the back door. "Okay, well, that's all I wanted to show you," I said. "I think I'll go over to Tommy's and see if he's home from church yet."

As I walked outside, the smile on my face was so big, you could have seen it a mile away.

Step Number Five—

Ad
Number
Two

I waited until Tuesday night before I started on Step Number Five: Put fake ad in paper from parents.

Since I already knew how to write a personal ad, this one was going to be the easiest step so far. All I needed to do was write a couple of quick lines and call it in to the paper by Wednesday afternoon.

I figured it wouldn't take much time, so after dinner, I watched a couple of TV shows. Then I took a shower and headed to my room.

Unfortunately, just as I pulled out my secret notebook, Robert pounded on my door.

"Oscar! Hey, Oscar, open up! I've got something I want to show you!" he shouted.

I didn't want to let him in, but if I didn't, he might get suspicious. So I shoved the notebook into my pillowcase and went to the door.

As soon as I opened it, Robert rushed into my room. He was carrying a mayonnaise jar with holes punched in the lid.

"Look, Oscar! Look what Franklin Brady gave me!" he said. "He just dropped it off at the house."

Robert held out the jar to show me.

I shrugged. "Spiders. Big deal," I said. "What's so exciting about spiders? You probably have more bugs than that living in your ears."

Robert looked insulted. "See, that just shows how dumb you are, Oscar," he said. "In the first place, spiders aren't *bugs*. They're not even members of the insect family, in fact. And in the second place, these aren't *ordinary* spiders. These are genuine *black widows*. Franklin borrowed them from his teacher. They're doing a science project at school."

I pretended to yawn. "Yeah, yeah. Sure they are, doofus."

Robert stood there a second. Then a sly little grin appeared on his face.

"Okay, fine. If you don't believe they're really black widows, I guess I'll just have to give you a closer look," he said.

Then, before I could stop him, he unscrewed the lid and turned the jar upside down on my floor.

"*There*. Now you can see them perfectly well," he said. He laughed and ran out of the room, shutting the door behind him.

I looked down. Black widows were taking off in all directions!

"Robert! Come *back* here! I *mean* it! You get these things back in the jar!" I yelled.

I started after him, then quickly stopped. If I moved, I would lose track of where the spiders were running. And the thought of not knowing where they were made me sick.

"MOM! DAD! COME QUICK! I *NEED* YOU!" I shouted.

That's when I felt it.

"OW!"

I looked at my foot. One of the spiders was running across the top of my big toe.

I froze in fear. "OH, NO! OH, NO! I'VE BEEN BITTEN BY A BLACK WIDOW! HELP! PLEASE! SOMEBODY CALL 911!"

I must have shouted for three or four minutes before my mother finally opened my door. By then, I was all shouted out.

"Oh, gee. I'm so glad that you could finally make it, Mother," I said sarcastically. "I'm sorry to take you away from your TV show, but I seem to be having a slight problem here. Nothing to worry about, really. It's just that I've been bitten by a deadly spider."

At that point, I lost track of the spiders and sat down on my bed.

My father came in. "Hey, hey, hey. What's all the hollering about in here?" he said.

I held up my foot. *"This,"* I said. "This is what the hollering's about, Dad. I just thought you and Mom might like to know that I won't be coming to breakfast tomorrow morning. I have a feeling that being dead takes your appetite away.

"Dead," I repeated. "D-E-A-D, dead. As in 'The boy is dead from a black widow bite.'"

I pointed to the bite mark.

"See it?" I asked. "See that little red mark there? That's the mark a black widow leaves after it poisons you to death."

My father shook his head. "A black widow spider? No. I doubt it, Oscar," he said. "I've lived here all my life and I've never even *seen* a black widow spider."

"Oh, well, then today must be your lucky day, Dad," I said. "Because there are five black widows running around in this room right this very minute."

Just then, a giggle came from the hall.

My father went out and pulled Robert into the room.

"Okay, let's hear it, Robert. What do you know about this?" he asked him. But Robert was laughing so hard, you couldn't make sense out of anything he said.

"He knows *everything* about it!" I said. "Robert's the jerk who set them loose in here. His friend stole the black widows from his teacher. And then Robert dumped them out on my rug!"

I tried to calm my voice. When you've been poisoned, it's probably not a good idea to use all your strength screaming.

I took some deep breaths. "Would anyone be interested in getting me to a hospital?" I asked. "Or would that make you people miss too much TV tonight?"

By now, Robert was laughing so hard, he seemed to be in pain, almost.

My parents couldn't take their eyes off of him.

I *had* to do something to get their attention back to me.

I gasped for breath and fluttered my eyes. "Mom? Dad? Are you still in here? Everything is getting hazy," I said.

That's when Robert totally lost it. He let out a loud hoot and collapsed on the floor.

"You dope!" he said between gulps of laughter. "Those weren't black widows. They were stupid little spiders from under our front porch."

My father was infuriated. He grabbed my brother by the feet and pulled him out of my room.

Robert was still holding his stomach. "Did you hear him, Dad? Oscar said that everything was getting *hazy*! What a dork!"

I wanted to crawl into a hole. I mean it. For a second, I almost wished I really *had* been bitten by a black widow. Anything would have been better than the humiliation I was feeling.

Mom glanced at my foot again. "Well, whatever kind of spider it was, it definitely bit you. I'll go see what I can find to put on it."

A few minutes later, she came back into my room carrying two cans. One was first-aid spray. The other was insect spray.

After she sprayed my bite with antiseptic, she took the insect spray and really let the spiders have it. She used the whole can, almost.

"There," she said finally. "That ought to kill them."

I coughed.

"*Them?* What about *me*? It smells terrible in here," I said.

"Oh, don't worry. The smell isn't harmful to *people,* Oscar," she said. "If you don't like it, just don't breathe for a while."

I looked at her strangely. "News flash, Mother. If I don't breathe, I die for sure."

My mother was quiet for a minute. Then, all at once, she hollered, "Robert! Come in here, please! *Now!*"

My brother showed up in the doorway. He must have thought that Mom was going to force him to apologize. Because he held his nose and said he was sorry. He was smirking when he said it, so it didn't count for anything.

When he turned to leave, my mother grabbed him by the back of his shirt.

"No, no, no. Hold it, buddy boy," she said. "I'm sure that you'll want to do more to help out than just say you're sorry. After all, because of you, Oscar has a painful spider bite and his room smells like bug spray."

Robert looked confused. "Yeah? So?"

"So go grab your pajamas and come right back," she said.

Robert started to argue, but my mother snapped her fingers. And if you're smart, you never argue with my mother after she's snapped.

Soon, Robert was back with his pajamas. He looked nervous as anything.

"Wh-what are you going to do to me?" he asked.

"I'm not going to do anything to you, Robert," said Mom. "I just thought it would be nice if you traded rooms with Oscar tonight. That way, he'll be able to breathe fresh air and get a good night's sleep. Sleep is very important when you're healing from a spider bite, you know."

She patted Robert's head.

"We really do appreciate this. Don't we, Oscar?" she asked me.

I grinned. "Oh, yes. We definitely do."

I went over to my bed and scooped up my pillow with my secret notebook still hidden inside.

When I got to the door, I waved.

"Nighty-night, *Spider-Man*," I teased.

Ha! What a great line!

After that, I went straight to Robert's room and wrote my second ad:

NEEDED: Temporary home for a wonderful boy.
555-6990.

Down the hall, I heard Robert cough.
I laughed out loud.

Step Number Six—

Getting Closer

The next morning, I put some extra money in my pocket. On the way to school, I stopped at a pay phone and placed my ad in the newspaper. I made the same arrangements to pay as before.

After that, it was four more days of waiting before I could move on to Step Number Six: Show ad to Hensons.

This time, the week went by pretty fast. Before I knew it, another Sunday morning had rolled around. For the third straight Sunday in a row, I asked my parents if I could take the paper up to my room after breakfast.

Unlike the week before, I had no trouble finding my ad at all. It was right at the top of page three.

I cut it out and put it in my pocket so I could take it down the street and show the Hensons. Then I went downstairs again and gave the paper back to my mother.

"Oh, good," she said as I handed it to her. "I wanted to take a look at the personal ads this week and see if there's anything else in there from the Hensons."

My heart stopped when she said that. Oh, my gosh! No! I could *not* let her see those ads. If Mom saw the hole that I'd cut in page three, I would never be able to explain it.

Quickly, I grabbed it back. "No, you *can't*," I said.

My mother frowned. "What do you mean I can't? Give that back to me. What's wrong with you, anyway, Oscar?"

"Nothing," I said. "Nothing's wrong with me. It's just that I already looked for another ad from the Hensons, and there isn't one, that's all."

Unfortunately, my mother is one of those people who always have to see everything for themselves. She reached for the paper again.

This called for drastic action.

Thinking fast, I bent down and started swatting the floor with it. Seriously. You should have seen me. I was tearing the paper up like you wouldn't believe.

Mom folded her arms and glared. She was definitely not happy. "What the H-E-double-L do you think you are doing?" she snapped.

I frowned. My mother almost never swears. I mean, I realize that she *spelled* the swear word this time. But even spelling a bad word is considered swearing, I think.

I used to keep a chart on the number of times she and my father slipped up and said a swear word in front of me. That way—if they ever heard me say a swear word—I could pull out the chart and show them that they aren't perfect, either.

I eventually gave up on the idea, though. Keeping up with my father's page became a full-time job.

I swatted the floor a few more times before I finally stood up.

"Geez, Mom. You didn't have to yell. You should be thanking me, in fact. Didn't you see that thing?" I asked.

"What thing? What are you talking about?" she said.

"I'm talking about that centipede-looking thing that was crawling up the front page of the paper," I said. "How could you not have seen it? It was *huge.*"

My mother shivered. She hates centipedes worse than anything.

"Are you kidding? There was a centipede?" she asked. "Oh, gosh, I'm sorry, Oscar. I just couldn't figure out what you were doing."

We both looked at the floor. The paper was lying there in shreds.

"Yeah, well, I'm sorry I tore up the paper, too," I said.

Mom shrugged. "Oh, well. I guess it doesn't really matter. You said that the Hensons didn't have another ad in there, right?"

"Right," I said. "I looked really carefully, too. I promise."

After that, I picked up the crumpled paper and walked to the back door. "I'll throw this out in the trash can," I said. "I was going outside, anyway."

Suddenly, Mom's face brightened. "Hey, I have an idea. Why don't you get Robert and the two of you can play some catch?"

I rolled my eyes. "No offense, Mother. But in case you haven't noticed, I don't care for Robert."

As I shut the door, Mom had already started another one of her talks on how "deep down inside," I actually love Robert.

I didn't go back.

A few minutes later, I walked up the Hensons' driveway. I was hoping that Mr. Henson would be in his garden, but I didn't see him anywhere. It was a pretty big disappointment, too. This meant that I would have to knock on his front door to get him.

And if there's one thing I can't stand, it's knocking on people's front doors.

For some reason, knocking on people's front doors makes me feel totally self-conscious. I never know what to do after I knock. Usually, I just rock back and forth pretending that I don't care if they come or not. But in my head, I'm secretly wondering if they're peeking at me through the curtains, hoping that I'll go home.

This time, though, it had to be done.

I forced myself to walk up to the screen door. I knocked hard. When no one came, I knocked again.

Finally, I heard footsteps.

"Why, hello there, Oscar! What a nice surprise," said a pleasant voice.

Oh, geez, no. It was *Mrs*. Henson. I needed to talk to her *husband,* not her.

"Oh. Mrs. Henson. It's you," I said. I leaned my head in the door. "Is Mr. Henson in there? Could he come out to play for a while, do you think?"

As soon as I said it, I felt my face heating up. What a stupid thing to say! *Could he come out to play for a while?* I mean, what part of my brain did that even *come* from?

Mrs. Henson laughed. "Wait here. I'll go see," she said.

I sat down on the porch step. If I had one wish in the whole world, I would wish that nothing dumb would ever come out of my mouth again.

As I sat there and waited, I prayed that Mrs. Henson wouldn't tell her husband that I had asked if he could play. I said an actual prayer to God, I mean.

After a minute, the door opened behind me. "Does someone out here want me to play?" said Mr. Henson, chuckling.

I looked up at the sky. *Thank you, God. Thank you very much. You just couldn't let it pass, could you?*

"Oh, um . . . hi, Mr. Henson. I didn't really mean *play,* exactly," I said. "I just wanted to talk to you for a minute, that's all. I hope I'm not bothering you or anything."

"No, of course not," he said. "What's on your mind, young fella?"

I shrugged. "Well, mostly I just wanted to

thank you for keeping the secret I told you the other day," I said. "I really appreciate having someone to talk to about it."

Mr. Henson put his arm around my shoulders. "Sure, son, sure. I've been thinking about you and your family all week. I really wish there was something Mrs. Henson and I could do to help you out. It upsets me to think you're going through such a bad time right now."

I nodded. "Yeah, and it's not getting any better, either, Mr. Henson," I said. "Have you read today's paper yet?"

He shook his head no. "That's just what I was doing when you knocked," he told me.

"Oh. Then I bet you haven't seen this yet," I said.

I took the ad out of my pocket and handed it to him. "I found it in today's personal ads."

Mr. Henson read it out loud. "'NEEDED: Temporary home for a wonderful boy. 555-6990.'"

His jaw dropped open. "Oh, no," he said. "You're not trying to tell me that your *parents* placed this ad, young fella?"

I nodded. "Yes, I am, Mr. Henson," I said. "That's exactly what I'm telling you. My parents are trying to find a nice family to take care of Robert until my father gets some of our money problems worked out."

Mr. Henson read the ad again. "And you're absolutely *positive* that it was your parents who put this ad in the paper, huh? This is your phone number, right?"

Just like before, I had been very careful about the phone number.

"Well, it's *almost* my number," I said. "The paper must have made a mistake and printed 555-6990 instead of 555-6999. But it's close enough, Mr. Henson. I'm sure that ad is from my parents."

I could tell by his expression that he believed me. It made me feel kind of bad, too. I really hated lying to a person as nice as Mr. Henson. But I had no choice. If I didn't get rid of Robert pretty soon, I would lose my mind.

After a few minutes of sitting there in silence, Mr. Henson finally got up. "Well, young fella, I hope you don't mind, but I think it's time for me to tell Mrs. Henson about this. My wife is very good at solving problems. Maybe she can think of a way to help."

I heaved a sigh. "Yeah, well, I guess that would be all right, Mr. Henson. But be sure and tell her not to mention any of this to my parents, okay? And she can't mention it to Robert, either. Poor little Robert. He's trying to be brave, but it's not easy."

Mr. Henson patted my arm. "Don't you worry, young fella. We'll figure something out. I promise. Everything's going to be okay. You'll see."

After that, he turned and went inside.

As soon as he was gone, I started grinning like an idiot. It was just so amazing, that's all. My plan was clicking along smoother than I ever imagined.

On the way home, I covered my mouth and laughed out loud.

Just two steps to go, and my life would be Robert-less!

Steps Number Seven and Eight— The Letters

I waited a few days before starting the next steps of my operation. I wanted to give the Hensons plenty of time to think about everything that I'd told them.

In the meantime, I made sure that my mother didn't forget about poor Mrs. Henson and her tired old back. In fact, I talked about Mrs. Henson dragging her husband around in his garden so much, I almost started believing the story myself.

By the time the week was almost over, I was more than ready to get on with Steps Seven and Eight: Write fake letter to Hensons and write fake letter to parents.

It was Saturday morning. I had an early baseball practice, but I rushed home as soon as it was over.

"Mom, I need to use the computer," I hollered as I ran in the door. "I have to do a report for school."

"Okay, fine," she hollered back. "But remember, it's not a toy, Oscar. And please don't mess up the printer like you did the last time."

My mother's memory is unbelievable. You get one crummy paper jam and it lives in her brain forever.

I went in the den and began to work. I was hoping that I would be able to write both letters by noon. But at 12:30 P.M., I was just finishing up the first one. It turned out pretty good, though, I thought.

> *Dear Mr. and Mrs. Henson,*
> *Our wonderful son Oscar told us that he's*

talked to you about our recent family problems.
Please don't worry about us. As soon as we get
rid of Robert, we will be able to rent out his room
and get some money coming in.

If you happen to know anyone in the neighbor-
hood who would like to have a nice little boy come
stay with them for a while, please let us know.

Yours truly,
Mr. and Mrs. Winkle

I printed it out and looked it over carefully. Since I had used my mother's best paper, it definitely looked like a grownup had written it. In fact, I was so happy about the way it had turned out, I decided to skip lunch and get started on the next letter right away.

Dear Mr. and Mrs. Winkle,
Your wonderful son Oscar told us that he
talked to you about our recent family problems.
Please don't worry about us. As soon as we find
a nice young man to stay with us awhile, we'll be
fine.

I only hope that my tired old back will
hold up a little longer so I can keep dragging
Mr. Henson around his garden.

Sincerely,
Mrs. Henson

P.S. Say hello to that cute little Robert for us.
Mr. Henson and I get such a kick out of that boy.

After I was finished, I folded both letters and put them in their envelopes. Then I hurried to my room and hid them under my mattress. I would "deliver" them on Monday.

When I went back downstairs, Robert was coming in the front door.

"Hello, Oscar the Grouch," he said.

"Hello, Robert the Slobert," I said back.

My mother ignored us. "How did practice go, Robert?" she asked, trying to change the mood.

Robert shrugged. "Not that good, really," he said. "I couldn't hit the ball at all today. My coach said I needed more practice. So I was wondering if you or Dad could pitch me some balls this afternoon."

Mom looked at her watch. "I can probably do it later," she said. "But right now I have to run to the store. And your father is cleaning out the garage."

She paused a second, then winked at him. "Maybe you could ask your big brother," she said. "I bet if you asked Oscar real nicely, he'd be happy to pitch you some balls."

I rolled my eyes to the ceiling. I hate it when my mother talks about me like I'm not even there. It's just insulting, that's all.

Robert turned to me. "Oscar, would you mind if we went outside and—"

I interrupted him. "I heard the question already, Robert," I said. "This may come as a shock to our mother, but I'm standing right next to you."

Anyhow, I figured Robert must really be desperate if he wanted me to help him. So I decided to be a good person and give it a try. The truth is, when Robert's trying to be human, I don't really mind helping him out.

The two of us went outside. As soon as I pitched him the first ball, I knew why his coach was upset. Robert had added some kind of weird dipsy-doodle to his swing that I'd never seen before.

He must have thought it looked cool or something. But he looked so ridiculous, I felt like laughing my head off.

I resisted the urge, though. If I laughed, Robert would just storm off. And if he ever used the dipsy-doodle during a real game, it would bring shame on the entire family.

I must have worked with him for over two hours that day. First, I made him choke up on the bat. Then I put his feet square to the plate so he couldn't swing so goofy. It took a long time, but at last he started getting some good hits.

When my mother got home from the store, she was so excited that we were still being nice to each other, she brought out a pitcher of grape Kool-Aid. I'm sure she got the idea from watching those corny TV commercials. But it was totally lame.

After she poured us each a big glass, she went into the kitchen and brought back cookies. As Robert and I ate them, Mom stood there smiling at us. It really creeped me out.

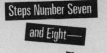

After I finished my last cookie, I went inside. Robert stayed out in the yard slugging down the rest of the Kool-Aid. When he finally came in, he had a purple stain all over his whole face, practically.

"Gross," I said. "There's a fungus among us."

Robert punched me in the arm. "Shut up, you Oscar Mayer wiener," he said.

Then he stuck out his purple tongue and went to his room.

To tell you the truth, I was sort of glad that things were back to normal between Robert and me. When Robert stays nice for too long, I start thinking that he's up to something.

Usually, I'm right, too.

I grinned to myself.

This time, though, *I* was the one with the plan.

Delivery
Day

I woke up Monday morning with a smile on my face.

"*Delivery* day," I said right out loud.

The end of Operation: Dump the Chump was almost here. It wouldn't be long before Robert would be packing his bags and moving out.

There were only three more days till school got out for the summer. To kill time, my teacher made us write a composition called "My Summer Plans."

While everyone else was writing about their exciting vacations, all I could think about was how peaceful my life was going to be without Robert the Slobert.

That afternoon, I rushed home and got the letter I'd written to the Hensons. I put it in my back pocket and told my mother I was going out to play.

Even from a few houses away, I could see Mr. and Mrs. Henson sitting on their front porch.

They waved as I walked up their sidewalk.

"Hi, Mr. and Mrs. Henson," I said. "I hope I'm not interrupting anything. But my mother wanted me to give this to you."

I took the envelope out of my back pocket and handed it to Mr. Henson.

He opened it right away and started to read.

I sat down on the step and waited for him to finish.

When he was done, his face was sadder than anything. "Oh, my. Do you know what this letter says, Oscar?" he asked me.

"Yes," I said. "My mom let me read it before I brought it over."

Mrs. Henson leaned over to see it, too. "What does it say, Ed?" she asked her husband. "Read it out loud. I don't have my glasses."

Mr. Henson sighed.

"Dear Mr. and Mrs. Henson,

Our wonderful son Oscar told us that he's talked to you about our recent family problems. Please don't worry about us. As soon as we get rid of Robert, we will be able to rent out his room and get some money coming in.

If you happen to know anyone in the neighborhood who would like to have a nice little boy come stay with them for a while, please let us know."

Mr. Henson looked at his wife. "It's signed 'Mr. and Mrs. Winkle,'" he said.

Mrs. Henson closed her eyes for a second. "Oh, no," she said. "Oh, dear."

For the next couple of minutes, no one said a word. Then all of a sudden, Mrs. Henson frowned a little bit.

She asked Mr. Henson to read the note one more time.

When he was finished, her frown got bigger. Something about the note was definitely bothering her.

"Is, uh . . . is something wrong, Mrs. Henson?" I asked.

Slowly, she shook her head. "No. Nothing's *wrong,* exactly, Oscar," she said. "It's just that your mother used the term 'get *rid* of Robert.' It just sounds a little harsh, that's all. Finding a nice place for your brother to live isn't the same thing as getting rid of him."

I felt myself start to tense. "Oh. Well, um, you just haven't been around my mother much, Mrs. Henson," I said. "She says 'get rid of' all the time. It's like a pet expression of hers, sort of. And besides, you should have seen how upset she was when she wrote this note. I bet she didn't even know what she was writing."

Mrs. Henson thought it over. "Yes. Of course. She was probably just upset."

It was definitely time for me to get out of

there. I stood up. "I'll tell you one thing, though," I said. "It really would be great if you guys knew someone in the neighborhood who could keep Robert. You know . . . like maybe if you knew an older couple who needed some help around the yard or something. That would be perfect, wouldn't it? I bet my parents wouldn't feel half as bad about getting rid of Robert if he was close to home and he was helping someone out. It wouldn't seem so much like charity, you know?"

I raised my eyebrows. "You guys don't happen to know any old couples around here, do you?" I asked.

Mr. Henson smiled, but he didn't say anything.

I walked down the steps and turned around. "Well, if you think of anyone, you can always call my mother," I said. "I mean, it's not like the deal with Robert is a secret anymore. So if you think of anyone who might like to have him live with them, you can call us right up on the phone. Like you could even call us tonight if any ideas came to you."

I paused a second. "Just remember one thing, though," I said. "If you do happen to talk to my father, don't mention the part about how he got fired from his job, okay? He's still very sensitive about that subject."

Mr. Henson stood up, too. "Don't worry, young fella," he said. "Mrs. Henson and I would never say anything to embarrass your parents."

"Great," I said. "Thanks, Mr. and Mrs. Henson. I always knew I could count on you guys."

I waved good-bye and headed down the sidewalk.

The minute I got home, I ran upstairs and grabbed the other letter from under my mattress. Then I rushed straight to the kitchen and shoved it at my mother. I needed to get her to read it before the Hensons called.

"Here, Mom! Open this, okay? I just came from down the street. Mrs. Henson asked me to give this envelope to you right away."

My mother opened it up.

As soon as she was finished, she put her head

in her hands. "Oh, my word. Those poor, poor people," she said.

"What?" I asked. "What does it say? Read it to me."

Mom picked it up again.

"Dear Mr. and Mrs. Winkle,

Your wonderful son Oscar told us that he talked to you about our recent family problems. Please don't worry about us. As soon as we find a nice young man to stay with us awhile, we'll be fine.

I only hope that my tired old back will hold up a little longer so I can keep dragging Mr. Henson around his garden.

Sincerely,

Mrs. Henson

P.S. Say hello to that cute little Robert for us. Mr. Henson and I get such a kick out of that boy."

My mother put the letter on the table. "Your father and I definitely need to talk about this when he gets home," she said. "There has to be something we can do to help them."

She looked at me. "I know you want that, too. Don't you, Oscar?"

"Yes, I *do,* Mom. I really, really do," I said.

Late that afternoon, when my father got home from the bank, I heard them discussing it in the bedroom. The door was closed and they were mumbling. But I could tell they were taking the situation very seriously.

What a *relief* it was to finally have all the steps of the plan over with. It made me nervous not knowing what would happen next. But whatever it was, I hoped it would happen soon. I couldn't stand to wait much longer.

That night at dinner, my parents started talking about the Hensons right away. It was a really good sign, I thought. They both kept looking at Robert and me and telling us how good it makes you feel when you help others.

Unfortunately, Robert didn't seem to be listening at all. Mostly, he just kept stuffing his face full of spaghetti and sloshing down milk.

Dad finally got tired of his bad manners and took away his milk glass.

"Robert? Have you been listening to anything we've been saying tonight?" he asked. "Your mother and I want to know what you and Oscar think we could do to help the Hensons."

Robert wiped his mouth on his arm. "The Hensons? Why do we need to help the Hensons?" he asked. "What's the problem?"

I stared at him in disbelief. For *days* I had been talking about all the trouble the Hensons had been having, and my jerky brother hadn't heard a single word.

"Man, Robert. Where the heck have you *been*?" I snapped. "Poor Mrs. Henson has a bad back and she needs someone to help her out for a while. Don't you hear anything that we talk about around here? You probably don't even know how much the Hensons like you, Robert. They talk about you all the time, in fact. They think you're just about the neatest kid in the whole world."

Robert made a face. "You're *kidding*. The Hensons *like* me? Why do they like me? I hardly even know them anymore," he said.

He cringed. "It makes me feel spooky," he said. "Having people like me who I don't even know. What if they're *stalkers*?"

Oh, geez. Robert was ruining everything. If I let him keep talking, my parents would give up on the idea of sending him down there. I had to find a way to shut him up.

I was seriously considering dragging him out of the room when, all of a sudden, the phone rang. I'm not making that up, either. It was just like in the movies. The timing was perfect.

My heart began to pound like you wouldn't believe!

This was the call I had been waiting for. I was sure of it!

My father answered the phone. Even though I could only hear his side of the conversation, it was better than I ever imagined.

"Oh. Hello, Mr. Henson. How nice to hear from you. We were just talking about you folks. How are you feeling this evening?"

My stomach did a flip-flop. I prayed that my father wouldn't ask anything personal. *No questions about Mrs. Henson's back. Please, please, please.*

"What's that, Mr. Henson?" my father said next. "Yes. Well, thank you very much. He and his brother have always liked you, too."

Yes! Perfect! This was the part where Mr. Henson was telling my father how much he and Mrs. Henson liked Robert! I knew Mr. Henson would find a way to bring up Robert without mentioning anything about Dad being fired.

Good old Mr. Henson. He was wording things so carefully, I was hardly even worried anymore. My father just kept smiling and nodding and saying, "Uh-huh, uh-huh."

Finally, Dad got ready to hang up. "Okay. Well, it sounds like a good plan to me, too, Mr. Henson. We'll finish talking about it here, and get back to you, okay? Bye."

After he hung up, my father looked at my mother and nodded. Then he looked at Robert and me.

Quickly, I stood up. I had to get out of there before my father gave Robert the old heave-ho. If I didn't leave the table, the shocked expression on

Robert's face would make me explode in laughter.

I ran up to my room as fast as I could. I almost didn't get there soon enough. The laughing started as soon as I hit the door.

"YEEEE-HAAAA!" I screamed into my pillow. "I did it! I did it! I really pulled it off! It's good-bye, Slobert Robert!"

Operation: Dump the Chump was a success!

The "chump" was officially *dumped*!

See You in September

After I finally settled myself, I went back downstairs to see what had happened. When I walked into the kitchen, Robert was nowhere to be seen.

My parents were cleaning up the dishes. Mom turned to me and smiled. My father did the same.

"Where did Robert go?" I asked.

I was almost positive he was off crying somewhere. The thought of it brought another grin to my face.

"He went outside for a little while," said my mother. "After we told him all the details about the Hensons, I think he needed to get used to the idea."

She came over and sat down beside me. "You and I need to talk about the Hensons, too, Oscar," she said.

I shook my head. "No, we don't, Mom," I said. "Honest, I already know exactly what you're going to say. And I'm okay with it, I swear. The Hensons need our help. And even though it's going to be hard splitting up our family for the summer, I know it's the right thing to do."

My mother hugged me. "You are *really* something, Oscar Winkle. Your father and I were so afraid that you'd be upset at the idea. Especially now that you're going to be an 'only child' for a while again. We thought you'd be so bored and lonely without Robert."

Bored? Lonely? Without *Robert*? Was she *kidding*?

I tried to act casual. "So, um . . . exactly what did Robert say when you finally told him?" I asked. "Did he take it okay?"

Mom nodded. "Yes, he took it great, actually," she said. "Of course, being an 'only child' is going to be a whole new experience for him, too, you know. He's always had you, Oscar. But I'm sure he'll get used to it."

"Yeah. I'm sure we both will," I said.

My curiosity was killing me. "Dad, exactly what did Mr. Henson say when he called?" I asked.

My father sat down next to me. "Well, he started off by saying how much he's liked you boys all these years. He told me that they had always dreamed of having grandsons like you and Robert. And then he asked if you guys liked to rake and help out in the garden."

Good old Mr. Henson, I thought to myself. *Good old _dependable_ Mr. Henson!*

"What else?" I asked.

"Let's see. After that, he said that they wondered if we would consider letting one of you boys come stay with them for a while. He never actually mentioned their medical problems. But I guess he just didn't want to seem too desperate."

Mom interrupted. "Do you know what I love

best about all of this, Oscar? I love it that Mr. Henson wasn't ashamed to ask us for help," she said. "He seemed to know that we were the kind of people he could count on. Neighbors helping neighbors. That really makes me feel good. Do you know what I mean?"

"Sure I do, Mom. Of course I do. I feel exactly the same way," I said.

My mother hugged me again.

Then, quiet as anything, she leaned over and whispered something in my ear.

My blood turned cold.

I swallowed hard and asked her to repeat it.

Mom smoothed my hair.

"I said that we're really going to miss you this summer, Oscar," she said. "We really and truly are."

The

End?

Don't ask me how everything got so messed up. It was the biggest disaster of my life.

I mean, where did I go so *wrong*? I must have asked myself that question a thousand times. Where in the world did Mr. and Mrs. Henson ever get the idea that *I* should be the one to come live with them? Didn't they listen to all the nice stuff I said about Robert? And what about how his room is better for renting than mine is? What's

wrong with the Hensons, anyway? Can't they hear? Maybe that's what happens when hair grows in your ears.

Still, that's no excuse for my parents. I've checked their ears. And neither one of them has any hair in there at all. I know they heard me tell them over and over again how much the Hensons liked Robert. Not me . . . *him*.

And why—all of a sudden—did my parents decide they have to help our neighbors? As far as I know, they've never helped out one single neighbor the whole time we've lived here. What a fine time for them to decide to be nice.

After my mother told me the news, I ran straight to my room to try and figure a way out of things. Right away, I ruled out telling the truth. I would rather spend the rest of my life at the Hensons' than let Robert know how wrong my plan had gone. If Robert knew the truth, he would never be able to stop mocking me. No. This was definitely not the time for honesty.

Finally, I decided to try *reverse psychology*. Reverse psychology is when you try to trick someone else into taking the punishment for you.

I found Robert out on the porch and called him into my room.

"Yeah? What do you want?" he asked with a smirk. "Shouldn't you be busy getting your rakes and shovels together?"

"Ha ha. Very funny," I said. "Go ahead and laugh if you want to, Robert. But it's a shame you have to stay in this boring old house this summer. It's too bad you won't be going away on a real vacation like I am."

Robert grinned. "Oh, yeah, Oscar," he said. "Spending the summer with a couple of old fogies sounds like tons of fun. If you're lucky, maybe next year Mom and Dad will let you spend the summer at a nursing home. I bet you'd *really* have a blast there."

He left laughing. So much for reverse psychology.

After he was gone, I racked my brain for more ideas, but nothing else came to me. After a while, I got so frustrated, I started to cry, almost. I mean, geez, how *depressing*. I was going to be spending

my summer in an old man's *vegetable* garden.

It was around eight o'clock when the phone rang again. I figured it was Mr. Henson calling back, wanting to find out if I was coming or not.

My mother answered it in the kitchen. I tiptoed halfway down the stairs and tried to listen. But when I couldn't hear, I went back to my room.

It's too bad I gave up like that, too. Because as my mother and Mr. Henson were talking, something in the conversation went wrong. *Very* wrong, I mean.

A few minutes later, Mom showed up in my doorway. The look on her face was downright scary.

Her voice was chilling, almost. "Mr. Henson is on the phone, Oscar," she said. "He wants to speak to you."

I swallowed hard. I just couldn't figure it out. What had happened to make her so furious?

I went into my parents' bedroom and picked up the phone.

Mom was right behind me. She was making me unbelievably nervous.

"H-hello?" I said into the receiver.

"Well, hello yourself, young fella!" said Mr. Henson, happy as anything. "Your mother just told me the good news. You're coming to stay with us!"

Poor Mr. Henson. He sincerely thought he was doing our family a favor.

"Oh, yeah, I'm coming all right, Mr. Henson," I said. "Thanks."

"Are you getting packed yet?" he asked. "Your mother said you could come this weekend."

I took a deep breath. It was really hard to act happy.

"No, Mr. Henson, I haven't started packing yet," I said. "But I'll definitely be there."

"Excellent!" said Mr. Henson. "Mrs. Henson and I sure are looking forward to having you here for a while, Oscar. By the way, how's your mother taking this? I hope I didn't say anything to upset her just now."

Oh, *no*. Just as I suspected. Mr. Henson had blabbed something he shouldn't have.

I glanced at my mother. She sneered.

"Um, exactly what do you think you might

100 *Barbara Park*

have said, Mr. Henson?" I asked quietly.

"Well, you told me not to say anything to your father about losing his job, remember?" he said. "But I thought it would be okay to mention it to your mother. So I told her that I used to be in banking myself, and that I'd be happy to try and help your dad get another job."

I looked over at my mother again. Her cheeks were completely sucked into her head.

Mr. Henson went on. "Listen, young fella. Before we hang up, I wanted to ask you if you'd like to spend the summer at our beach house. It's just a small place, but it's right on the ocean. We usually go for most of the summer. Do you think your parents would mind if we whisked you away for that long?"

This time, I didn't even *have* to look at my mother. "Oh, believe me, Mr. Henson," I said. "Right now, I doubt that my parents would care if you whisked me away for the rest of my life."

He chuckled. "Good," he said. "I'll give them all the details later. Meanwhile, Mrs. Henson and I will see you in a few days, okay? I think she's going to bake one of her delicious cherry pies to celebrate."

Somehow, I managed to say, "Oh, boy."

After I hung up, my mother followed me back to my room.

I wasn't sure whether she had figured out my whole plan. But she definitely knew a *lot* more than I ever wanted her to.

I sat down on my bed and shook my head.

"Oh, man, that crazy Mr. Henson. He really gets some weird ideas in his head, doesn't he?" I said. "Like—for some reason—he thinks that Dad got fired from his job. Isn't that funny?"

My mother said, "Ha ha."

I kept on talking. "It's weird the way old people get confused about stuff sometimes, don't you think?" I asked. "I mean, it's probably a *good* thing that I'll be staying with the Hensons for a while. That way, I'll be able to help him if he gets confused about anything else."

My mother crossed her arms. "How very lucky for them," she said dryly.

Finally, I walked over to the doorway and turned out my light. "Okay. Well, I guess I'd better

be getting some sleep now, Mom. Tomorrow is a school day, you know," I said.

I gave her a quick kiss on the cheek and got into bed.

But instead of leaving, my mother just kept standing there in the dark.

I propped up on one elbow. "Uh . . . is something wrong, Mom?" I asked.

"Wrong?" she repeated. "Wrong? Oh, heavens no, Oscar. What could possibly be wrong? It's just that before I go, I have one little question for you, that's all."

"One little question?"

"Yes, Oscar," she said. "Its something I'm curious about."

Her voice got suddenly louder. "*How stupid do I look?* Huh? Tell me. Exactly *how* stupid?"

Oh, wow. She was even angrier than I thought.

"Answer me," she insisted. "Answer the question, Oscar."

My heart started to hammer.

"Um, uh . . . h-how stupid do you look?" I stammered. "Well, let's see. It's kind of dark in here, so I really can't see your face that good at the moment."

Mom turned on the light. "Well, I certainly hope that your eyesight improves over the summer, Oscar Winkle," she snapped. "Because when you come home from your stay with the Hensons, if I still look stupid to you, we'll take you to the eye doctor. Because believe it or not, I am *not* an idiot, okay?"

I nodded as fast as I could.

My mother continued. "I don't know all the details of what you did, Oscar," she said. "And to tell you the truth, I don't even *want* to know the details. If I knew the whole story, I'm sure I would be even madder than I am right now. And if I was any madder, I would have a complete melt-down."

I raised my hand to interrupt. "Maybe we should talk about this tomorrow, after you've had a chance to calm down," I suggested.

"Tomorrow?" Mom asked. "*Tomorrow?* Oh, no, Oscar. Tomorrow, you and I are going to be way too busy to talk. As soon as you come home

from school, we're going to have to start packing. It takes a long time to pack when you're going to be away for the whole summer. And believe me, Oscar, you really *are* going. For some reason the Hensons think they're doing a wonderful thing here. And I wouldn't let them know that you tried to make fools of them for the world."

There was no sense arguing. I took a deep breath. "Mr. Henson wanted to know if I could go to the beach with them this summer," I said.

"*Not* a problem," my mother said. "The beach would be perfect, in fact. I think putting a little distance between you and me is the best thing for both of us right now."

She turned off the light and stormed down the hall.

As for me, I just lay there, unable to even close my eyes. I didn't sleep that whole night, in fact. I mean, how could I, you know?

The next day at school, I was groggy and depressed. But depressed or not, when I got home, my mother did exactly what she'd said she would do. She brought the suitcases to my room and we started to pack.

I'm finally beginning to accept it. I'm spending the summer with the Hensons. And that's that.

Meanwhile, Robert the Slobert is going to day camp. I was going to go, too, but now that's definitely off. Not that I really mind that much. Last year at camp, Robert got us kicked out of boating class. The first time he got in our rowboat, he stood up and pretended he was George Washington crossing the Delaware. The boating instructor blamed both of us and she made us sit on the dock for the rest of the week.

Speaking of boats . . . I wonder if the Hensons have a boat? If they don't, maybe they would take me on one of those deep-sea cruises for a day. That might be kind of fun, actually.

I mean, the thing is, I've always liked the beach pretty well. And there's almost always a couple of lonely kids looking for someone to play with.

Maybe I'll ask Mom if I can take our good canvas raft. She's still pretty mad at me. But not as mad as she was that first night. Today, she went to

the store and bought me all this good-grooming stuff to put in my suitcase. Like she just brought in a dumb little manicure set for my fingernails, for instance.

Hmm. Look at the tiny little scissors in this thing. Maybe I could show them to Mr. Henson. I'll bet they're the exact size for snipping off those ear hairs of his.

That reminds me. I wonder what Mr. Henson does with his false teeth when he swims. I hope he doesn't take them out and leave them on the blanket. I'm not sure I could take that.

Speaking of swimming, I'd better find my bathing suit. And maybe I should get my Frisbee, too. Mr. Henson isn't too old to toss a Frisbee around, I bet.

Hey. Who knows? Maybe this summer will turn out better than I thought. After all, I guess a whole entire summer without Robert can't be *all* bad.

The problem is, he'll still be around when I get home again.

Oh, man. If *only* I could get rid of Robert

during the school year, I'd have it made. It's such a shame the kid doesn't go to boarding school somewhere.

Boarding school?

Whoa. Wait a minute! Why haven't I ever thought of that before?

Boarding school just might be the answer I've been looking for!

All it would take would be a little planning. I could work on it this summer. I *know* I could.

I'll plan every single detail . . . one step at a time.

Boarding school! Yes! I'm a genius!

Let's see now. . . .

Where did I put my secret notebook?

If you liked Barbara Park's *Operation: Dump the Chump*, then you'll *love* her Geek Chronicles trilogy!

The Geek Chronicles #1:
Maxie, Rosie, and Earl—Partners in Grime

Meet Maxie, Rosie, and Earl— three kids who unite as they await their doom at the principal's office. Shy Earl is there because he refused to read out loud in class. Nosy Rosie is in trouble because her teacher is sick of her tattling. And then there's Maxie, who finally got tired of being teased and took matters into his own hands. Now they wait like sitting ducks. But no matter what the outcome may be, these three bumbling outlaws have just begun the start of a memorable friendship. . . .

"Park does it again. Here's a book so funny, readers can't help but laugh out loud."
—*Booklist*

Available wherever books are sold!
ISBN: 0-679-80643-1

The Geek Chronicles #2:

Rosie Swanson: Fourth-Grade Geek for President

Sure, Rosie Swanson wears geeky glasses and tattles on her classmates. But, hey, snitching has its good side. Thanks to her, Ronald Milligan has stopped blowing his nose in the water fountain. And now Rosie is determined to do even more for her classmates— by becoming president of  the fourth grade! With the help of her two best (and only) friends, Maxie and Earl, Rosie devises a brilliant campaign to defeat the two most popular kids in her class: soccer star Alan Allen and model-wannabe Summer Lynne Jones. But when Alan steals Rosie's slogans, it's time to watch out. Nosy Rosie is on the warpath!

"Right on target . . . a very good read."
—*Booklist*

"As bright and funny as they come."
—*Kirkus Reviews*

Available wherever books are sold!

ISBN: 0-679-83371-4